The Dog of Knots

The Dog of Knots

Kathy Walden Kaplan

Eerdmans Books for Young Readers
Grand Rapids, Michigan / Cambridge, U.K.

©2004 Kathy Walden Kaplan

Published 2004 by Eerdmans Books for Young Readers

an imprint of Wm. E. Eerdmans, Publishing Co.

255 jefferson Ave. S.E. Grand Rapids, Michigan 49503

P.O. Box 163, Cambridge CB3 9PU U.K.

Printed in the United States of America

04 05 06 07 08 09 7 6 5 4 3 2 1

Library of Congress Cataloging-in-Publication Data

Kaplan, Kathy Walden.

The dog of knots / written by Kathy Walden Kaplan.-- 1st American hardcover ed.

p. cm.

Summary: In Haifa, Israel at the onset of the 1973 Yom Kippur War, nine-year-old
Mayim struggles with questions about her future, particularly mandatory service in the Israeli
army, but finds comfort in friends, relatives, and a very old, stray dog with no name.

ISBN 0-8028-5259-9 (Hardcover : alk. paper)

1.   Jews—Israel—Juvenile fiction. 2. Israel-Arab War, 1973--Juvenile fiction. 3.
Israel—History--1967-1993--Juvenile fiction. [1. Jews—Israel—Fiction. 2. Dogs—Fiction. 3.
Israel-Arab War, 1973--Fiction. 4. Israel—History--1967-1993--Fiction.] I. Title.

PZ7.K12935Do 2004

[Fic]--dc22

2003011492

For Jonathan, Ariel, and Paul
—*K. W. K.*

Chapter One

"Where are you going?"

"To the window, Grandfather."

"And now?"

"Now I am waiting."

"Can I wait with you?"

"Oh yes, Grandfather."

Mayim's grandfather joined her at the window.

"We will see him through the gate."

Rehov Margalit curved down from the main road in Haifa along the hill next to the wadi.

"Should we go outside?" asked her grandfather.

"He's very shy. He doesn't know you. He might run away."

"So we'll wait inside."

When Mayim smiled at her grandfather her blonde ringlets wiggled by her ears. Her grandfather stroked her cheek.

A moment later a face appeared in the gate. A brown nose sniffed the air, and seeing Mayim at the window he took a step into the courtyard.

"Grandfather! This is him."

"Oh, he's, he's . . . all knotted up."

"Those are ringlets, ringlets like mine, Grandfather. He looks like me, except he's a dog. Isn't he wonderful!"

Mayim's grandfather stared at the large, rosy-beige dog whose every inch was covered with tangles of thick, heavy knots.

"He doesn't look like he is being very well cared for."

"Oh, Grandfather, he doesn't belong to anybody. He lives down in the wadi. Every morning he comes up to Chaim the butcher who gives him his breakfast.

"He's the butcher's dog."

"Chaim says not. And then he walks past our house on his way back to his home in the wadi. A few people on the street leave out dishes with leftovers for him, too."

The dog wagged his tail as he looked at Mayim and her grandfather. Even his tail was covered with tangled knots.

"Hello. What a fine old dog you are," Grandfather said, following his granddaughter through the door to the patio.

"Mayim, see how white the fur is around his mouth? This must be a very old dog. White hair even in his eyebrows." Grandfather cupped the dog's chin in his palm and with his other hand moved a few tangles to better see the dog's clear brown eyes.

"Have you given him a name?"

"Grandfather, I have tried several different names, but he never pays attention to any of them."

"Well. Old Dog, someone of your age must have had at least one name."

"I think he forgot his name," Mayim said.

"Let's give him our own name. How about Rover?"

"That's silly."

"Prince?"

"With all his knots?"

"Have you thought of any?"

"I like Knotty."

"Or the other one—Naughty."

"Oh, grandfather, he is never that kind of naughty!"

"I can see that. He is a very dignified and noble dog. Perhaps if you call him Knotty a few times he will accept it as his name."

"I am going to give him some cheese. He loves cheese." Mayim ran into the kitchen and came back with a plate of white goat cheese.

"He eats that?"

Mayim laughed. "He especially likes stinky cheese!"

After the dog finished the plateful of cheese, he smiled, wagged his tail, and went back out the gate to the sidewalk.

"He doesn't really live in the wadi, does he?"

"Yes. He sleeps under a rocky shelf almost all the way down."

"You can see this place from the road?"

"Well, Grandfather, almost," she stammered.

"Did you go all the way down into the wadi?"

"One morning I went down before school. It was sunny. There were no clouds in the sky. I was sure it was safe. I followed him part of the way back down after he visited Aunt Yula."

Grandfather shook his head.

"I was very careful. I didn't go all the way down, and I never left the path. I came right back up. It was all right."

"Mayim, does your mother know you went to the

wadi?"

"No, Grandfather. Please don't ever tell her."

"I want you to promise me that you will not go down there again."

"I promise, Grandfather, but really nothing could have happened. Please don't tell Mother."

Mayim's grandfather smiled and put his finger up to his lips.

Chana, Mayim's mother, called from the door. "Come. Eat."

Chapter Two

In the morning the Hamseen, the hot wind from the desert, blew. Mayim hated walking to school in the wind. The sky was dirty orange. Everything smelled bad. The wind made everybody out of sorts. Mayim was already out of sorts. Her grandfather had gone back home to Jerusalem leaving Mayim and her mother alone again.

The wind blew strong at her back. Wondering if it would hold her up, she leaned against it. It didn't, and she almost fell backwards on the steep hill. Thinking the wind might be stronger on the other side of the street she crossed over just as the vegetable seller stepped down onto the street from Mrs. Koslovsky's walkway.

"Shalom, Mayim," he said. Mr. Saludi, the vegetable seller, walked down her street every morning carrying a dirty gray bag over his shoulder. This morning bright yellow grapefruits poked up through the hole in his bag. "Do you think your mother might want some?" he asked.

"She might. She hasn't gone to work yet," Mayim answered the old Arab. His scrabbled gray beard was the same color as his gray bag. He wore an old suit jacket over his baggy, dark pants.

"I will call and ask," he said, starting across the street. He called out as he passed each house, and Mayim loved the sound of his musical voice.

"Wait!" called Mayim. "I want to ask you about the dog! You know—the knotty dog."

"He lives in the wadi. He belongs to no one."

"I know, but do you know his name?"

Mr. Saludi laughed. "I think he's too old to have a name."

"How can that be?" Mayim asked.

"It is a mystery."

"How old is he?"

"Older than you."

"Okay, I knew that. But what do you call him?"

"It doesn't do any good to call him. He answers to no name."

"I knew that, too. But do you have a name for him?"

"I do."

7

"What?"

"I call him Laffah—coiled like a pile of rope next to the boats down in the harbor.

"I like that. Maybe I'll call him Laffah."

"He doesn't come to it. He comes to no name."

"I could try."

"You should hurry on to school now, Mayim."

"Oh! I forgot! See you later!"

•　　•　　•

After school Mayim stopped by at the corner market to buy a few cups of yogurt for her mother. On her way home she noticed Mrs. Koslovsky outside in her garden so she ran up the steps to see her.

"Good afternoon." Mrs. Koslovsky smiled.

Mayim loved when Mrs. Koslovsky spoke English. She sounded so perfectly and wonderfully English, but really she was from Russia. Her parents were on their way to America when they ran out of money in England. "For the lack of fifty pounds sterling I grew up English instead of American," she used to tell Mayim.

"My grandfather went back to Jerusalem," Mayim said.

"Did he now?"

"Yes, but we will get to visit him very soon, Mother said."

Mrs. Koslovsky picked up a few empty dishes from under the bushes. "Well, come along. I have those special cookies you like so much."

Mayim followed her into the house, and Mrs. Koslovsky put the cups of yogurt in the refrigerator to keep them cold.

"I would be happy to wash out the kitty dishes for you," Mayim said.

"You're such a dear. While you do that I'll make us some milk-tea to go with our cookies."

Mayim washed and stacked up the dishes.

"I think we should have our tea in the living room like proper ladies," Mrs. Koslovsky said.

Mayim collected Mrs. Koslovsky's papers and books from her table and put them on the piano. The doors to the patio were open, and the late afternoon light from the Hamseen made the room seem very warm.

Mayim looked up at the curved sword over the doorway. In the bright light she could see the ornate patterns carved into the silver scabbard. The sword had belonged to the king of the Bedouin, and he had given it to the doctor who had saved his people from a plague of small pox. It was the finest thing he owned, that sword—a priceless gift to the young doctor who had been Mrs. Koslovsky's new husband. When her young husband died he left Mrs. Koslovsky the sword and the wonderful story that went with it. She often said it was the finest thing she owned. Mayim was never sure whether she meant the sword or the story.

"Here we go," said Mrs. Koslovsky, putting the tray on the round table.

"Do you want me to open the package of cookies?"

"Please, then everything will be ready for our afternoon tea."

Mayim opened the package, and the rectangular vanilla biscuits split apart from each other. She put four on the dish.

"Four? You only want two?"

Not wanting to appear greedy, Mayim nodded.

"All right then. We can start with two."

Mayim waited until Mrs. Koslovsky put a cookie into

her mouth before picking up her own.

"I spoke to the vegetable seller this morning. Mr. Saludi says that the name he gave the knotted dog is Laffah."

"Laffah?"

"Laffah—coiled like a rope," she said.

"That's good. Sounds like laughing."

"I didn't think of that. It does."

"He brings him bread, you know," said Mrs. Koslovsky, picking up her cup of tea.

"Mr. Saludi?"

"Yes. I've seen him slip him a piece from inside his bag of fruits and vegetables."

"I guess everybody feeds him. He's really a sweet dog. Did you give him a name?" Mayim suddenly thought to ask.

"The old dog? Oh yes. I give all the wild animals names."

"I still remember the name you gave the cat with the emerald eyes—Prosciutto. It sounds so foreign."

Mrs. Koslovsky smiled before she sipped her tea. "It's Italian."

11

"What does it mean?"

"It's a very tasty deli meat."

"Deli meat? That's silly. What kind?"

"Oh, one that's dried," said Mrs. Koslovsky, concealing a smile.

"What name did you find for the dog?"

"I call him Bailey. When I was your age that was the name of the policeman who made his rounds on our street in England. The dog makes his trip up from the wadi every day to visit all his friends and to check on the neighborhood. In a way he reminds me of that old policeman."

"Bailey is a wonderful name. Better than the one I gave him—Knotty."

"Knotty is a fine name; but myself, I like Laffah."

"Mr. Saludi says he doesn't answer to it."

"Well I'm not surprised. He doesn't much like Bailey either."

"Where do you think he came from?" Mayim asked, looking out the window.

"He has always lived in the wadi, ever since I came to Haifa."

"But didn't you come a long time ago?"

"Oh, my, yes. Right after my husband died. A few years after the war."

Mayim wanted to ask which war—there had been so many—but she didn't want to make Mrs. Koslovsky remember her husband. She didn't want her to get sad again, so she suddenly blurted out, "How could he possibly be so old?"

But it was too late. Mrs. Koslovsky's memory was slipping right out the window, right in front of Mayim's face.

"Two is not enough!" Mayim shouted.

Mrs. Koslovsky turned her face toward Mayim and regarded her with a very calm smile. "I told you it wouldn't be."

Chapter Three

Mayim held all the yogurt cups with her left arm as she opened the door. The house was dark and empty. Sometimes she loved being the first one home in the afternoon, but not this day. She put the yogurt cups away in the refrigerator and opened the door to the back patio. From the railing she could see the blue waters of the Mediterranean down the hill and beyond the edge of the city. She knew her mother missed Jerusalem, but she loved the sea. She, herself, had been tiny when her father died during the last war. It was the only memory she had of Jerusalem, playing with a top in the late afternoon with the sun coming in sideways. Her father wrapped the string around the top and spun it for Mayim. Mayim squatted down to watch the humming top spinning on its point.

In her mind she did not see her father's face. The face in her mind was one from a photograph. There was no memory except that one in her mind. She had been a year-

and-a-half old that afternoon, her mother said, amazed that she remembered something from when she was so tiny. She didn't remember being told her father had died. The day the movers came to their apartment and carried all their things down the stairs was the beginning of the stream of her life where the memories were all connected.

It was the moving man letting down her crib on a strap from the balcony. It swung free from the railing on a long leather strap the moving man gripped in his teeth as he lowered it to the garden below. It had shocked her to see such a thing. After they moved into the house on Rehov Margalit those teeth were the hard bit of sand her life built itself upon, her memories built upon each other, layer by layer, like the shiny layers of the oyster pearl.

A cool breeze blew up from the water lifting Mayim's curls. From the road she suddenly heard her mother's car.

"Ima!"

"Mayim!" Her mother waved from the car.

"Ima, I got the yogurt. It's in the refrigerator."

"Wonderful," her mother answered, putting down a bag of books. She looked like a college student instead of a professor.

"What did you teach your students today?" Mayim asked.

"Covalent bonds. One of the ways electrons hold atoms together."

"Do they understand?"

"They understand the words. I doubt they understand the implications."

Mayim giggled. "I understand."

"Oh. You do."

"Yes, Ima, covalent bonds are like this." She threw her arms around her mother's waist and buried her face against her stomach. "Your arms have to go around me, too."

"Mayim! You're right! How did you know?"

Mayim wouldn't tell. Sometimes she looked into the big chemistry book her mother taught from. She understood a lot from looking at the pictures even if she couldn't understand all the words.

"What did you learn today?"

"We made electricity with batteries. It was boring."

"Mayim, boring!"

"The needle just moved up and down."

"When electrons jump from one atom to the next, that's what makes the needle move. Moving electrons are electricity."

"Electrons are electricity?" Mayim asked, incredulous.

"Yes."

"The teacher just said it was current."

"Now you know better. It is not boring. I thought you liked science."

"Science is my favorite subject!" Mayim protested. "But mostly I like learning about animals, that part of science."

"Electricity is what makes muscles move in all the animals you love. It is important to learn about."

"All right. Mrs. Koslovsky gave me tea and cookies this afternoon."

"Did she?"

"You know what she calls the dog who lives in the wadi, the one I named Knotty?"

"What?"

"Bailey."

"Do you want to help me make dinner?"

"Okay."

Mayim crumbled matzo crackers into a bowl. Her mother coated pieces of chicken with egg and then the cracker crumbs and put them in the frying pan. Schnitzel was Mayim's favorite meal.

"Can I slice the cucumber instead of the tomatoes?"

"What about the onion?"

"Oh, Ima, you do the onion. I am afraid the knife will slip."

Mayim sliced the cucumber as thinly as she could. She could never get the slices paper-thin like her mother's, but she worked slowly and thoughtfully. Smelling the cucumber as she sliced it was her favorite part. Her mother's slices tasted better, but if her mother sliced them she would miss out on smelling them.

"How long did it take you to learn how to slice them the right way?" Mayim asked when she was finished.

"Every time I slice them I have to figure it out as I go."

"What?"

"It takes me four or five slices. Each cucumber has its own shape, its own density. And the skin makes a big difference in how you cut it."

"But you do it so fast. It looks so automatic."

"Speed is from practice. It is never automatic. You can never take your mind off the knife and daydream about something else. That's when you cut yourself."

"Hmm," Mayim murmured, remembering slicing apples and cutting herself just at the moment her mind pushed out to sea.

•   •   •

After her bath, before bedtime, Mayim's mother read her a story.

"How long before we go to Jerusalem to see Grandpa?"

"Soon. Aunt Yula wants you to come to her house after school tomorrow. She has made strudel, and she wants you to have some."

"Okay. I just wish she would put a little more sugar in the strudel."

"It's sweet enough."

Chapter Four

Not sweet enough, Mayim thought with her mouth full of apples. It was not a subject to discuss with her Aunt Yula, however.

"How is it?" Aunt Yula asked.

"Delicious." Mayim smiled.

"Do you want another piece?"

"Ima said I could only eat a little or it will spoil my dinner."

"Okay, you eat and then help me with my homework."

Aunt Yula was Mayim's great aunt. She was the school nurse at the high school during the day, but during the night she was a college student studying English literature. She piled her schoolbooks on the kitchen table.

There was a scratch at the kitchen door.

"Oh," sang Aunt Yula. "It is my friend."

She opened the door, and the knotted dog walked into the kitchen.

"Hi," Mayim said, slipping him a bit of strudel.

"I have your dinner waiting on the stove," Yula said. She scooped a stew of rice, peas, and carrots into a bowl and put it on the floor.

"I didn't know you gave him dinner."

"The butcher gives him meat, but a dog is like us. He needs to eat everything. So I give him his vegetables."

"Mrs. Koslovsky calls him Bailey," Mayim said. Mrs. Koslovsky and Aunt Yula were best friends.

"His name is not Bailey."

"Mr. Saludi calls him Laffah."

"Ridiculous."

Mayim laughed. "It means coiled, like a rope."

"He is more than his fur. I think he has a great heart. I decided to call him Adel, my dear Adeleh."

"What does it mean?" Mayim asked.

"It's a Yiddish word, and it means noble and gentle."

"Noble and gentle," Mayim said to herself. "That really suits him. Just when did you see him the first time? Mr. Saludi says he is very, very old."

"It's hard to remember exactly. It was after I came back from the American University in Beirut. After I was married. After the boys were born. But I was still young. You know, I am not exactly sure. But Mr. Saludi is right. He is very, very old."

Mayim hoped Aunt Yula would talk about her years in Beirut. From Haifa it was only a hundred miles, but it might as well have been in another galaxy. It was a world closed to Aunt Yula since the last war, closed to all of them. Aunt Yula always spoke of it wistfully, always spoke of the people with such fondness. "We used to go to each other's homes to celebrate each other's holidays," she had told Mayim once. She tried to imagine Mr. Saludi coming to dinner at Passover or going to his home and feasting after Ramadan, but such thoughts only made her nervous and sad.

"Are you going to go to Jerusalem with us to see Grandpa?" Mayim asked.

"Too soon to make a decision," she answered. "Jerusalem is a long way. I have my homework for my class." She gave the dog a bowl of water.

•   •   •

The sun was slipping into the ocean as Mayim rounded

the sharp corner between Aunt Yula's street and Rehov Margalit. She stopped on the sidewalk and watched the sun's light make a path across the sea right into her eyes.

A damp nose touched her hand. It was the dog. She let her fingers go between the thick tangles down to the skin. It was soft and warm like a puppy's. After a moment the dog went on down the street to the opening in the low stone wall by the wadi. As he disappeared down the path Mayim crossed over to see where he had gone. The path curved in and out on its way down the hillside. The dog disappeared behind the trees planted along the path.

The golden undersides of the clouds turned dark rose as the sun finally disappeared into the soft blue sea. And below, in the flat land beyond the wadi before the shore, electric lights suddenly lit up the low white buildings of the tank factory.

"Good night, Adel," Mayim called after the dog.

Chapter Five

"Are you ready?"

"Yes, Ima. I just need to get the strudel Aunt Yula made for Grandpa."

Mayim and her mother reached the plain below Haifa before the sun came up. They came to the coast road and made a left turn on the road south. They passed fields with rows of young banana trees, their long leaves bright. Mayim didn't see any bananas. Maybe next year they would be old enough. They passed small towns with small, square, white houses growing under rows of eucalyptus trees.

Mayim put her head on the car window and fell asleep.

"Look how beautiful the hills are this time of year," Chana said.

Mayim straightened up and looked around. The brown hills rolled like waves into and out of each other. "We're almost there."

"You slept a long time."

Mayim looked out from all the windows at the scrubby hills. To the left she saw rising from the bushes a circular cement enclosure, the remnants of an old water tower or a watch tower. Bullet holes broke its surface. Mayim tried to imagine the soldiers shooting at each other, some inside, some outside the cement walls, but her mind wouldn't go there. As her gaze passed back across the road she saw the Egged bus heading straight for them.

"Ima! He's not going back!"

Chana hit the brakes as the bus swerved towards them. The bus had come around the curve passing another car, but it came too fast and the momentum kept it from going back to its own lane.

Mayim screamed.

Still braking, Chana pulled the car all the way off the road. The blue and white bus did not slow down.

Chana's car slid through the gravel into a ditch and stopped.

"I would like to put my hands on his throat," her mother whispered, gripping the steering wheel.

"Why do those stupid bus drivers have to drive like

that!" Mayim shrieked.

"I don't know. I hate them." She put the hand brake on, stepped out of the car, and walked to Mayim's side.

Mayim looked down into the ditch. "Can we get out?"

"One tire is in the air. Maybe. Let me try."

She got back into the car and turning the wheel sharply pulled backwards onto the roadway.

Mayim stopped shaking by the time they saw the city.

•   •   •

Grandpa's apartment building was on the road next to the old city. Like the others it was constructed of pink rocks. In the past when she saw the pink rocks they made her laugh. This time she didn't laugh. She couldn't wait to get inside, to be in Grandpa's arms. Mayim stumbled against the door and pushed it open.

"Grandpa, the Egged bus driver tried to kill us!" Mayim shouted, standing in the doorway.

"What?" Grandpa picked Mayim up off the floor.

"It's not enough they get paid more than anybody else in the country," Chana said following Mayim into the apartment. "They act like nobody has a right to be alive but them."

"He ran us right off the road, Grandpa," Mayim cried.

"Oh my. We can report it. Did you get the bus number?"

"Bus number? I was just a little too busy getting out of his way to take note."

"We went into the ditch, Grandpa," Mayim added, her mouth quivering at the corners.

"Don't cry. Don't cry."

Mayim put her face under Grandpa's neck. She thought she would cry, but the tears didn't come. How could she cry when she was in her favorite place in the world—Grandpa's arms?

"Let me sit down, Mayim. You have grown too much for this old man." Grandpa ran his hand over Mayim's hair. He started counting. "One, two, three . . . they are all here; not one ringlet is missing."

"You're silly, Grandpa!"

"I am glad you are all in one piece. And the car?"

"No damage," Chana said, putting down a string bag on the kitchen table. "Yula made you some strudel. I asked her four times to come with us, but she wanted to work on her English papers."

"I hoped that she would enjoy a change of scene."

"Since Aaron died it is very hard for her to change her routine at all," Chana added. Aaron was Yula's husband. He had died after heart surgery two years earlier. Grandpa and Aaron were brothers.

"I'll see her in a few weeks. She doesn't have to change her routine."

"Are you going to come to Haifa?" Mayim asked.

"For the holiday," he answered.

"Mayim, get down now," Chana said. "You'll break Grandpa's lap."

"I will not!"

"Mayim. Guess who has come downstairs three times already this morning to see you," Grandpa said, smiling.

"Uri!"

"Yes. Uri has some things he wants to do with you today."

"What things?"

"Go upstairs and ask him."

Chapter Six

Uri was three years older than Mayim. He was her best friend. They met on the stairs.

"Mayim, do you want to go to the Old City today?"

"By ourselves?"

"Why not?"

"My mother won't let me."

"Could you ask? Your grandfather thought she would agree, if I came with you."

"We wouldn't be safe there alone."

"It will be fine. It's been months since there have been any troubles. Besides, we are only going just inside the gate. There is a shop I want to show you."

"What kind of shop?"

"It will be a surprise."

Mayim was stunned when her mother gave her permission to visit the Old City with Uri.

Mayim and Uri got on the bus outside the apartment

building.

"Aren't you afraid?" Mayim asked.

"No. It is our place. Moshe Dayan announced last week that we will begin construction on a new hotel on the West Bank."

"What did the Palestinians say?"

"They didn't say anything. There aren't going to be any more wars. Everything is settled."

Mayim folded the thoughts over in her mind and put them away. Peace. No more wars. There, it was settled.

They entered the Jaffa Gate and followed the narrow path around a few corners past many shops full of drums, carpets, and lanterns made for the tourists.

"This is the shop," Uri said, stepping inside. "I found this necklace last month, and I have been saving money to buy it for my mother's birthday."

"Hello, Uri," said the shopkeeper.

"This is my friend Mayim from Haifa. I want her to see the necklace."

The shopkeeper gazed at Mayim while taking a box from behind the counter. He slipped off the top and handed the box to Mayim.

"Uri, your mother will love this. It's beautiful!"

"It's real gold. And the stone is very special."

"It's so blue!"

"It's an Eilat stone. Most Eilat stones are green, but this one is blue."

"Are you going to buy it today?" the shopkeeper asked.

"Yes," Uri answered. "I just wanted to make sure Mayim liked it, too."

"I do like it, Uri, and so will your mother."

Uri paid for the necklace.

"There is a restaurant just around the corner where they make the best shawerma in the world. Are you hungry?"

"Yes!"

At the restaurant the waiter was sharpening a long knife on a ridged metal rod. In front of him a pyramid of layered lamb turned steaming over a rack of glowing coals. The wonderful smell of spices and lamb drifted up and down the road. Uri and Mayim ordered from outside the restaurant. The waiter moved the meat vertically and sliced the cooked portions into a pita filled with shredded lettuce.

"Tehina?" he asked Mayim.

She nodded.

"Harif, hot sauce?"

"Just a little."

They turned back towards the gate, eating as they walked.

"Now that you are twelve do you think your parents will let you come on the bus to visit us in Haifa?" Mayim asked.

"I am sure."

"That would be so much fun. There is really a lot to do in Haifa. We could go down to the city to go to the movies. We could go hiking down in the wadi. If she would let me come to the Old City with you, my mother would let me go to the wadi with you. You could meet Knotty."

"I'll ask my parents. Do you want to go down to the Wall? It's only a little bit farther?"

"But Uri, we told Grandpa that we were only going just inside the gate. I don't want to get in any trouble. I've been to the Wall, and it's a long walk from here."

Uri shrugged. "I forgot. You have to be good. You're still a little girl."

"That's not fair!"

"A good little girl," Uri complained.

"I'm not going to the Wall no matter what you say."

"Then I'll go by myself," Uri said, taking a turn to the left.

"Fine. Have fun." Mayim watched him disappear around a corner. She hesitated a moment and then went on toward the Jaffa Gate by herself. When she reached the Jaffa Gate she turned around. Uri stood just behind her.

"Are you mad at me?" he asked.

"You left me alone in the Old City!"

"No, I didn't."

"Yes, you did!"

"It was only for a minute. I came right back. If you had turned around you would have seen me."

Mayim didn't speak to Uri on the bus. She didn't say good-bye in the hall outside her grandfather's apartment. She wanted to tell on him, but if she did when Uri came to Haifa her mother wouldn't trust him. There would be no movies, no hiking in the wadi.

"Did you have fun with Uri?" Chana asked.

"Oh, yes, and you should see what he bought for his mother's birthday—the most beautiful necklace in the world."

Mayim finished up her homework during hafsakat tzo-horayim, while her mother and grandfather slept. Mayim loved this time of the day when everybody was either asleep or very quiet and she could listen to the world. She closed her book and walked to the edge of the balcony. She was sure she could hear all the birds in the city talking to each other, saying good evening to the sun. From the hills behind her, the sun stretched out underneath the clouds and lay its long-fingered rays across the city drawing evening up like a shimmering coverlet.

"It's beautiful, isn't it?" asked Grandpa.

"It's my favorite time of day," Mayim answered.

"Mine, too. Did you finish your homework?" Grandpa asked, putting his arm across Mayim's shoulders.

"Yes! Finally! Grandpa, what should I be when I grow up?"

"You should do what you love."

"Is that what you did, Grandpa?"

"I love plants and growing things. I love watching the life in them change with the warming days. I love seeing apples growing on the trees. But when I was young there

34

was a country to be made. I had other skills and the country needed me to do those other things. When I was asked to help run the government I felt it important not to let anyone down," he answered with sadness.

"Shouldn't I do what you did, do something for the country, something that's important?" Mayim asked.

"The most important thing a country needs is for all her people to do what they love, to do it with all their hearts. Then it will be like spring, when all the hills are covered with millions of smiling wildflowers, each their own color."

"And you know what else, Grandpa?"

"What else, Mayim?"

"All the birds will be singing, too."

Grandpa hugged Mayim. "And an old man will listen and his heart will smile."

"Look at the city now," Mayim said. The golden roof of the Dome of the Rock was almost red in the last rays of the sun. "Uri says it's our place now."

"That's his father talking. The Arabs will never let go. They can't let go any more easily than we can let go."

"Do you argue a lot with Uri's father?"

"Oh, Mayim, everybody in the government argues all the time."

"Isn't it hard to live in the same apartment building with someone you argue with?"

"Yes, of course."

"I don't care what Uri says. He's my best friend. I won't argue with him."

Chapter Seven

After a light supper Chana and Mayim kissed Grandpa good-bye and started back for Haifa. At the crossroads Chana stopped for two soldier girls waving for a ride.

"Shalom. Thank you for picking us up," one girl said as they climbed into the back seat. "I'm Talya and this is Ronit."

"Isn't it late to be traveling?" Chana asked.

"We stayed too late at my parents' house. Momma always cries when I leave," Talya replied.

"Are you going back to your unit?" Mayim asked.

"Not just yet. We will spend two days with Ronit's family in Naharia and then we will go back," Talya answered.

"Where is your unit?" Chana asked.

"On the Golan. We have another month there and then we'll go south to the Negev. Where are you going?" asked Ronit.

"To Haifa. I'll go through Naharia so I can drop you

off. It will be too late for you to get another ride."

"You don't have to do that," said Ronit.

"You think I could sleep tonight if I didn't?" Chana asked.

"That's very kind of you."

"I haven't forgotten what it was like to be a soldier."

"What do you do now?" asked Ronit.

"I teach chemistry at the Technion."

"You make enough money to have a car?" Talya asked.

Chana laughed.

Mayim's mouth opened and out popped the words, "We have a villa."

"Mayim!" Chana shouted.

"We do," Mayim said, embarrassed. She was always taken aback how total strangers could ask such personal questions. This time her resentment had gotten her wedged into a corner.

"You can buy a villa on a professor's salary?" Ronit asked. "Maybe I should go to college, the way Momma says."

"You should go to college," Chana answered. After a silence she added, "The house belonged to my husband's

38

family. After he died it came to me."

"I am sorry your husband died."

"He died in the Six Day War," Mayim added. "In the Sinai."

"I am so sorry."

They drove on through the dark hills. The moon came up, and before long it reflected back as they reached the sea.

"Do you like the army?" Mayim asked.

Ronit answered no. Talya answered yes.

"I wonder if I will like the army," Mayim said, half to herself.

"You won't," Ronit answered.

"Don't tell her that," Chana said.

"It's a big adjustment having to spend your days doing what someone else wants you to do," Talya said. "But you get out of your parents' house, you get to meet new people. I think you will like it."

"Maybe I'll get an exemption," Mayim said.

"You can't get an exemption," Chana said.

"Religious girls don't go to the army," Mayim answered.

The two soldier girls smiled at each other.

"It won't work. You are not from a religious family," her mother answered.

"Maybe I'll go to nursing school!" Mayim shouted. "Then I can have an exemption."

Talya and Ronit laughed out loud.

"Why are you laughing?" Mayim asked.

Talya answered, "Because almost every single girl in Israel has the same argument with her mother."

"And her father," added Ronit laughing. "So many hours we shouted and shouted, my father and I. And in the end I went to the army."

"Why don't you like the army?" Mayim asked Ronit.

"My boyfriend is a student at the University of Haifa. I don't get to see him enough."

"It's only two years," Chana said.

"Two years! Do you know how many other girls he can meet in two years?" Ronit cried.

"So, he will meet them whether you are in the army or not," Talya said.

"I will ask for an exemption," Mayim stated.

"You will go to the army," Chana answered.

Ronit and Talya settled back against the rear seat and were quiet until they reached Naharia.

"The next time you are on leave, come visit us," Chana said to the girls. "We live at 14 Rehov Margalit."

• • •

On the way home after school Mayim thought about the army. She tried to imagine herself eighteen years old and in a uniform. She could imagine the uniform, but she had no idea what she would look like. By eighteen she would be twice as old as she was now. She tried to imagine all the things that would happen between now and then, but nine years from now was as far away as the moon.

At Mrs. Koslovsky`s house she dropped her book bag on the cement step next to the patio and rang the bell.

"There's my girl."

"Good afternoon, Mrs. Koslovsky," Mayim said in her best English.

"I would ask you to come in, but I forgot to stop at the butcher shop on my way home."

"I'll go back. What do you need?"

"A bit of meat for the cats and for Bailey. The butcher always has a packet ready on Sundays. Let me give you some money." She gave Mayim one Israeli pound and ten grush.

"It won't take very long." Mayim ran up the steep hill to the main road and across the street to the butcher shop.

"Mayim!" said the butcher, smiling.

"Shalom, Chaim."

"What can I do for you?" he asked, his blue eyes shining.

"Mrs. Koslovsky needs her cat meat. Here is the money."

"I have her package just here, in the refrigerator," Chaim said, handing the paper-wrapped package across the counter. "We can't have the cats going hungry."

Mayim laughed. "What would we do without Mrs. Koslovsky's cats?"

"I'll tell you exactly what we would do without them. Before you moved here the city decided there were too many wild cats, so they poisoned them."

Mayim gasped in shock.

"And then you know what happened?"

42

Mayim, speechless, shook her head.

"All the rats came up from the docks. Before, the cats were everywhere, and then the rats were everywhere. Going out in back to put something in the trash became an exciting adventure."

"Then what happened?" Mayim asked, surprised that her mouth would make words.

"The city decided that the cats were good for something after all. Isn't that stupid? They brought more cats to the city after that."

"What about Knotty? Was Knotty here then?"

Chaim smiled. "Don't worry. They don't know about the dog. We aren't going to tell anybody anything about Knotty. He is our special friend. He is our special secret."

"I'll never tell!" Mayim blurted out. She took the package and started for the door. "Was Knotty here then, when the cats were poisoned?"

Chaim nodded.

"Mrs. Koslovsky calls him Bailey."

Chaim smiled. "I call him Havi. It's a nickname. From chaver, friend. He was my first friend when I came to Haifa."

"When was that?" Mayim asked.

The butcher gazed out the window looking back over time and nodded his head. "Long ago, Mayim, long ago. Give my regards to Mrs. Koslovsky."

Mayim raced back to Mrs. Koslovsky's with the cat meat.

Chapter Eight

"Mrs. Koslovsky, were you here when all the cats were poisoned by the city?"

"Let's not talk about that," Mrs. Koslovsky answered sadly. She took the package. "You can set our places for tea and I'll get this stuff cooking."

"I can cook the cat meat," Mayim said.

Mrs. Koslovsky opened the paper wrapper. Feet. Chicken feet. With toenails. And chicken heads. With beaks. "You need to wash them and put them in the pot with a little salt."

"They eat this?" Mayim asked.

"Well, you can't expect a cat to live on bread and milk. Besides, I save a little for Bailey, too. He is very fond of chicken."

Mayim wished she hadn't offered, but she couldn't make a fool of herself by saying no after she had said yes. She rinsed the feet off quickly and threw them in the pot.

All the heads were crowned with red combs. When Mrs. Koslovsky took the plates into the other room Mayim looked more closely at one of the heads. She pried the eyelids apart and looked into the gray eyeball. She washed the feathers on his head a second time and threw him in the pot.

"Don't forget the salt."

"Oh."

"And Mayim, put the lid on a little askew and set the heat at medium."

"Okay," Mayim answered, relieved that the chore was finished.

They sat down to tea with the late afternoon sun coming in from the street.

"So how was Jerusalem?"

"I went into the Old City with Uri to buy a necklace for his mother."

"And your grandfather?"

"I think he's okay. Maybe a little tired. Mrs. Koslovsky, do you think I would make a good soldier?"

"Absolutely."

"Were you in the army in England?"

"I was in the Air Force, the Royal Air Force, during World War II."

"Why did you go into the Air Force?"

"I wanted to go into the Navy, but to be in the Navy your family has had to have lived in England for two generations."

"Were you a pilot?"

"No. The first time I climbed up on the wing of an airplane for a mission, I slipped and broke my leg. I sat out most of the war, until the end when I helped bring Jews out of the camps. Yes. That was tough for a girl of nineteen." Mrs. Koslovsky gazed straight into Mayim's face.

Mayim was hoping she would think of something to say, but there were no words.

Mrs. Koslovsky went on. "Later on I helped smuggle refugees into the country at night. We sneaked past the British and dropped them off on the beaches. Those were very exciting times to be in this country."

"We brought two soldier girls to Naharia last night. They were going back to their unit on the Golan. I don't want to be a soldier."

"Really? By the time you are eighteen you will want to

go with your friends. You will feel differently then."

"Why did you go to fight the war?"

"I had to help stop Hitler. We all had to do our bit. Winning the war took all of us working as hard as we could. If the Germans had won we wouldn't be sitting here having tea, my dear."

"Maybe there won't be any more wars when I'm eighteen," Mayim suggested.

"Maybe. The Arabs lost Jerusalem last time. No telling what they might lose the next time. Some people say they would never dare strike us again."

"They wouldn't, would they?" Mayim asked.

"An old lady like me knows you can never predict what the future will bring to us. And that is why we have to have an army. Just in case. After all, the Turks might decide to reconquer the area." Mrs. Koslovsky laughed.

"The Turks." Mayim laughed.

"It's time to take the meat out of the pot," Mrs. Koslovsky said, putting her tea cup on the table. She stood up.

"Okay," Mayim said reaching for another cookie.

"Okay?" Mrs. Koslovsky asked, waiting.

"What?" Mayim asked.

"Come on. You need to do this part, too."

"There's more?" Mayim whined.

"Up!"

Mayim followed reluctantly. Mrs. Koslovsky poured the cooking water into a shallow dish. "Now you take the tongs and fish out the pieces."

Mayim put the heads and feet on a plate.

"They can't eat the toenails. And when you finish taking off the toenails, pull the beaks out of the heads."

Mayim pulled the sharp toenails from the gelatinous chicken toes. She had to use the tongs to pull the beaks loose.

"This is disgusting."

"Yes, but the animals can't digest those things. You want to take dinner out to Prosciutto and her friends?"

"What about the bones?"

"They can eat the bones. Besides, if we don't give them the bones, they'll just get them out of the trash anyway."

Mayim took the dishes out to the garden. Prosciutto was at her feet instantly, mewing and curling her tail around her knees. In a minute four other cats arrived, grabbed a foot or a head and hid under separate bushes to eat.

"Good. Now you'll know how to take care of the cats if I ever get sick and have to go to the hospital."

Mayim looked at the tall, muscular woman. "Sick? Are you going to get sick?"

"You never know," she answered, winking.

"That's not going to happen," Mayim said.

•   •   •

"Ima, guess what I did today."

"There you are," answered Chana. "Aunt Yula called to talk to you."

"I was at Mrs. Koslovsky's cooking the cat meat," Mayim said proudly.

"Mrs. Urlansky called Yula to say Uri will be coming on the train to see you this weekend."

"Why didn't she call me?"

"You weren't home. Yula told Mrs. Urlansky we would go down to the Ir to the train station to make sure Uri finds the Carmelit."

"That's not hard. Why doesn't he find his own way?"

"Mrs. Urlansky is a good mother, but maybe a little over-protective of Uri. The problem is that I have a faculty meeting. I can't go down to the city. You will have to go down to meet him."

"By myself?" Mayim asked, amazed that her mother would consider such a thing.

"Yula said she can't get away either. I think you can do this."

"Oh, I can do this," Mayim answered, ready for the adventure.

"Also, Yula said she would be happy if Uri stayed at her house."

"What!"

"She has the extra room."

"He's my friend. He's going to stay here with me."

Chana smiled. "I tried to be tactful."

"What does that mean?" Mayim asked.

"Tactful means that I found a way to say no without hurting Yula's feelings. I told her that you and Uri had been planning every detail of this visit for at least a year and that Uri might be very unsettled with any changes of plan."

"So he's going to stay with me?"

"Yes, Mayim."

Chapter Nine

Mayim took the bus from Rehov Margalit past the Super Sol in the Merkaz HaCarmel. An old woman with a cane got on at the next stop. Before she got to her seat a group of rowdy high school students pushed her aside. One took the seat she intended for herself. The old woman grabbed onto the pole to brace herself as the bus pulled out into traffic.

"Ich bin ein-und-achtzig!" she shouted in German, waving her cane at the boy. "Ich bin ein-und-achtzig!" (I am eighty-one! I am eighty-one!)

Two of the high school students persuaded their friend to get up and let the old woman have his seat.

At the Carmelit Mayim left the bus and boarded the train that burrowed its way underground down through Hadar, the middle level of Haifa, down to the Ir, the old part of town where the city had been originally built around the port. Mayim walked past the old stone buildings and peered around a corner. She couldn't believe the fragrance that came from that wet and dirty alley. Beyond a doorway, she saw the hot ovens. It was the pita factory and the odor of baking bread caressed her face. She stopped a moment to enjoy it, and a young boy appeared from behind the ovens carrying a wooden tray of unbaked pita. When their eyes met they both smiled, happy to share something so precious.

Around the corner Mayim almost walked into a horse. He was pulling an empty cart from the vegetable market. Mayim put a hand out to touch his neck, but she pulled it away quickly before his owner noticed.

A group of Arab men, their heads wrapped in red and white checked keffiyahs, sat outside a small restaurant around a tiny table drinking coffee. On the next block a restaurant offered falafels to people passing on the street.

"You want a falafel?" a man called to her, teasing the young girl and smiling.

"Not now, thank you," she answered, not missing a step as she bolted across the intersection.

• • •

The train pulled in just as Mayim reached the station.

"Uri!"

"Mayim! So this is Haifa," Uri said, shifting his pack to his other shoulder.

"I came all by myself to get you," Mayim announced proudly.

Uri patted her on the shoulder. "Good for you. Good for you."

"It's a few blocks to the Carmelit. Do you want me to help carry something?"

Uri passed Mayim a plastic sack. "Mother made a cake for you and Chana."

Workers on their way home crowded the Carmelit. Uri and Mayim had to stand the entire ride to the Merkaz. Since the buses in the Merkaz were full, Mayim flagged down a sherut, a taxi. Two other people inside moved over to make room for Mayim and Uri. At the Super Sol the driver stopped to pick up one more passenger carrying four sacks of groceries. At Rehov Margalit the driver let them off. Mayim paid the fare and the sherut drove on toward the University.

On the patio of the old people's home several old

women were gathered, reminiscing with each other in their rocking chairs.

"Shabat shalom, Mayim," an old lady with silvery white hair called out.

"Shabat shalom, Mrs. Singer. My friend, Uri, has come here to visit me from Jerusalem. Uri, this is Mrs. Singer."

They stepped onto the patio and Uri shook Mrs. Singer's hand.

"I am glad you can come to visit our Mayim. She is alone too much of the time. She needs to spend more time with young people her own age."

"The other girls on the street don't like me very much."

"That's their misfortune," Mrs. Singer said. "I saw your mother's car go down the street."

"We need to go then. Have a pleasant Sabbath, Mrs. Singer," Mayim said.

"You never told me that the girls here don't like you," Uri said as they continued down the street.

"They all grew up here. They have known each other since they were in gan yeledim together. I am from Jerusalem. I am a stranger here."

"But you have been here a long time."

"It doesn't matter, Uri."

"It will be better later on. When you go into the army you will all be equals."

"The army!" Mayim said with exasperation.

"What?"

Mayim sensed an argument if she said what was on her mind so she changed the subject. "Did you bring your shoes for hiking in the wadi?"

Uri nodded. "Wait a minute." He caught Mayim's arm and pulled her to a stop.

"Excuse me," said a bearded Hasid wanting to get past them into the small synagogue.

Uri let go of Mayim to let the man pass between them.

"Come on. Mother will want me to help make dinner," Mayim said and quickly turned down the steep hill to her house.

Chapter Ten

"Uri." Chana kissed the boy on both cheeks. "I am so glad you could come."

"Haifa is so different from Jerusalem," he exclaimed. "Even the air and light are different."

"Come, let's put your things in Mayim's room. She has offered to take the couch."

"It's really pretty in my room when the sun comes in the first thing in the morning," Mayim said, pointing to the large double window.

"In the morning, the first thing, even before the sun comes up, we will go out on our expedition," Uri said, eyes bright.

"Come to the balcony. You can see the wadi from there," Mayim said.

They looked down the steep wadi across the ridges to the south.

"What is that they are building?" Uri asked, pointing to

the large cement building on the horizon. A crane perched over it like a heron stepping through water.

"That's the new hospital. They have been working on it forever. You can see just over there the path that goes down into the wadi."

"By the road?"

"Yes, but then right after that hill the path stops. That is where we can begin our expedition. I have seen Knotty go down from there, and I am sure we can find some of his footprints."

Mayim, Uri, and Chana ate their meal at a table out on the balcony as the sky darkened. A man's voice rising and falling in song threaded its way through the trees from the synagogue.

"Can I get you some more mitz eshcoliot?" Mayim asked Uri.

"Sure."

Mayim poured the grapefruit syrup from a bottle and added seltzer.

"I see why you like it here so much," Uri said to Mayim. "The sea is beautiful."

"It almost makes up for not being in Jerusalem, but not

quite," Chana said, slicing more pieces from the challah. "How are your parents? You know, I sort of miss all the arguments we used to have."

Uri looked surprised. "My parents are fine. My father is very busy. He said there might be a strike." Uri's father worked for the Histadrut, the labor union. When Uri and Mayim were smaller their families spent long hours into the evening arguing about labor politics. Sometimes Uri's father or Mayim's father would lose his temper and begin shouting. Mayim would cry and Uri would plead with them to stop. Chana or Uri's mother would take the children off to bed, and the arguing would go on until the stars turned in the sky. There would be a few hours of peace and then the day would begin.

Uri asked Mayim, "Do you remember the arguments our parents used to have?"

"No. Did they argue?" Mayim looked at her mother.

"Of course we argued. How else does anything get sorted out?" Chana said. "Listen, all my classes had first exams today and I don't want to have to grade all of them tomorrow so I am going inside now. I'll let you two take care of the dishes. Okay?"

"Okay," Mayim answered, a small whine in her voice. Uri ate another piece of challah.

"Do you really remember my father?" Mayim asked.

Uri nodded. "I was five then, when the Six Day—" He was going to say war, but stopped himself, not wanting to make Mayim sad. "I was five. They used to fight a lot. Sometimes your grandfather would come and then it was worse."

"I wish I could remember my father. I don't think it's fair that you get to remember him and I don't."

"Let's go down to the path on the wadi."

"We can't go down there in the dark."

"Just at the street, at the beginning. I want to see what it looks like at night."

A warm dry breeze rose up from the wadi and touched Uri's face. "Look, Mayim, there is a ship. What are all those lights below?"

"The tank factory."

"Do you want to walk back up to the Merkaz?"

"Okay."

As they passed the synagogue people came out to the sidewalk. The last one locked the door. They passed the old people's house. Mrs. Singer was sitting in her rocking chair next to a thin, feeble man.

"Good evening, Mrs. Singer."

"Mayim, come here. I want you to meet Mr. Cohen. He arrived here this evening. He is going to live here now with us."

Mr. Cohen stretched out a thin hand with long fingers to greet Mayim and Uri, but he didn't rise from his chair. "Good, good," he said.

"We are on our way to the Merkaz," Mayim told Mrs. Singer.

"Come see us tomorrow. Mr. Cohen plays the piano and sings beautifully."

At the main road they considered whether to take the bus and decided to walk. People came out of their homes. The buses filled up and the street was noisy with traffic.

At the Merkaz they stopped at an outdoor restaurant and both ordered Cokes. "Let's go down to Hadar and see a movie," Mayim suddenly suggested.

"But it's late."

"It's not late."

"Call your mother and ask her."

Mayim ran to the telephone and slipped in a slotted token. When she came back she was smiling.

"She said yes?" Uri asked.

"If we promise to do all the dishes when we get back."

•   •   •

The Carmelit down to Hadar was packed with young people. Uri and Mayim came to the street with theaters with the flood of people. The sidewalks were too narrow for everyone and most of the people walked in the street. The young men wore very tight pants and their tight shirts were open halfway down their chests. The girls laughed, all beautiful. Some walked in tight pants, some with long legs bare for everyone to see. Everyone smoked cigarettes. Mayim wished she had worn something else; she felt like a baby in her shorts. Uri began to move like the other young men, shoulders swaying, very self-confident.

They found a movie, a western. In spite of the signs, nobody put out their cigarettes and the theater was smoky.

After the movie Mayim took Uri down the street. "We can get a bus from here that will take us straight to our street. We don't have to go back on the Carmelit."

The house was quiet when they returned. They washed the dishes quickly and went to bed eager for their hike in the morning.

Chapter Eleven

Mayim opened an eye and listened. The city was still asleep, but the birds were waking up in the pale blue light. She crawled from her bed on the couch and dressed.

"You made breakfast!" Mayim said, standing in the doorway of the bright kitchen.

"Finally. I thought you were going to sleep all day."

"Why didn't you wake me up?"

"I wanted to finish making breakfast and packing our lunches, then I was going to wake you up," Uri answered.

They ate the scrambled eggs, toast, and tomato-cucumber salad quickly. Mayim and Uri left Chana a note on the kitchen table. "She needs to sleep in one day a week," Mayim said. They put the lunches into their knapsacks and quietly left the house.

On the street Mayim found herself skipping for joy in the dawn light. Uri ran along beside her, laughing. They descended into the wadi along the paved path. At the end of the path Mayim stopped.

"This is the way Knotty comes up the wadi."

Uri looked at the steep rocky path and shook his head. "We'll slip if we go that way. It's too steep. Let's go sideways along that ridge of rocks, and maybe we'll be able to find our way down by zigzagging. That's what we do in the scouts when we are climbing mountains."

"Okay," Mayim answered, following Uri. He moved carefully over the loose rocks and through the dry shrubs. They stopped to watch the sun rise behind them.

"We should be able to see Knotty when he comes up," Uri said.

"I am sure he is already at the butcher's waiting for breakfast," Mayim answered.

"This early?"

"Chaim told me Knotty is always there the first thing."

Uri moved along the ridge until he found a place in the rocks they could brace their feet against to make a narrow descent. They crossed back across Knotty's footpath and made their way down a steep crevice. Uri turned as Mayim's foot slipped on a loose rock. She slid down the crevice in a tumble of rocks and dust. He grabbed her knees and stopped her slide.

"Are you okay?" he asked.

Mayim stood up, brushed off her shorts. "Yes," she answered, embarrassed and a little shaky.

"Let's go on."

They made four more zigzags across the dog path until they came to a spot where it was less steep. Then they followed the path straight down until it turned south along the curve of the mountain. As the path passed over a small hill, it turned back to the other side of the wadi. When they were about half-way down the wadi they stopped and ate lunch.

"Look," Uri said and pointed to a lizard sitting on a rock a few feet from Mayim's knapsack. At the movement of her head he skittled away.

Uri laughed. "If I lived here I would come down here every day."

"I wish mother would let me."

"Of course you can't come here alone. You're a girl."

"That isn't why," Mayim protested. "When it rains the water runs down the mountain and floods the wadi."

"What about Knotty? What does he do when it floods?"

"I don't know," Mayim said, annoyed at herself for not knowing, annoyed at Uri because he found out she didn't know.

"Let's go on."

They followed a path to the top of a small ridge. The ridge was formed by large rocks, and the path was no longer obvious. They walked along the rocks looking for a way down.

"Look," Mayim said, pointing at a cleft.

"Be careful," Uri said.

Mayim sat on the rock and slid down the cleft. At the bottom of the cleft she stood up. "This is it."

"I can't see you," Uri said.

"Just come down the way I did."

Uri scooted along the cleft. It made a sharp turn, and he jumped down to where Mayim was kneeling.

Part of the rock jutted out creating an overhang. Beneath was a small cave.

"This must be where he sleeps," Uri said, looking into the cave.

Mayim picked up a handful of dog hair. "This is Knotty's."

"What a great place to live," Uri exclaimed.

"The water would never reach him out on this ridge."

"Or the rain."

"But how does he get back up again. How are we going to get back up again?" Mayim asked, looking back at the steep cleft in the rock they had just slid down.

Uri tried climbing back up the cleft, but he could find nothing to grasp. "I guess we could let ourselves down and come back around . . . wait." Uri stepped on the other side of the rocky overhang. Wedged tightly together, half a dozen rocks formed a staircase up the side of the overhang.

"Look at this. We didn't see it from the top," Uri said, scrambling up. "This is obviously the way Knotty comes." He easily climbed back down and joined Mayim on the ledge in front of the cave.

Mayim and Uri crawled back into the cave. Beyond the opening the cave went back five or six feet into the mountain. There was only room for the two of them, shoulder to shoulder.

"If he came all the way to the back he would still be warm on the coldest winter day," Uri said.

They crawled back to the opening and sat on the ledge, looking at the sea.

"What a front porch!" Mayim exclaimed.

Uri took two apples from his knapsack and gave one to Mayim.

"This would be a great place to come and daydream. What do you want to be when you grow up? Are you old enough to think about things like that now?"

"You are so mean. Don't you remember yourself at nine?"

"Of course."

"It doesn't sound like it. You had daydreams when you were nine."

Uri nodded. "I'm sorry. I just think of you as being much, much younger than I am, or was. Maybe it's because you were still a baby when you moved away."

"And you were really grown up! A whole five years old!"

"I had started school and you were still in gan yeledim. I'm sorry. Please don't be mad at me. Tell me about your daydreams. What do you see yourself doing when you are grown up?"

"It's hard. I mean, I love animals. Grandpa says I should do what I love the most. I especially love birds. Maybe I could study birds."

"Then you could have a chicken factory."

"A chicken factory! I don't want a chicken factory!"

"Chickens are birds. And it's what the country needs. If you don't like chickens, maybe you could learn all about turkeys and raise turkeys."

Mayim was so angry she thought about shoving him over the ledge. Instead she counted to ten the way Aunt Yula taught her and said, "I'd rather have a fish farm."

"That's even better."

Mayim had to count to ten a second time. Deciding not to argue with Uri was easy to think about. It was very hard to actually do.

"What are you going to do when you grow up?" she asked, dropping her voice a little sarcastically at the last two words.

Uri's mind had moved ahead of her question, and he didn't notice her sarcasm. "I think I might like to stay in the army."

"What?"

"If they let me. If I am good enough. The country needs me to be a soldier. Someone has to stop the terrorists."

"Isn't there something else? Something you love?"

Uri shook his head.

"I don't believe you."

"Believe me."

"Uri, you are so good at math. I thought you wanted to teach mathematics."

"The army needs soldiers who are good at math."

"The country needs teachers just as much. Does your mother know you want to stay in the army?"

"No! And don't say anything to her, either. When the time comes and I'm older it will be easier for her. Then she will understand."

"Is that what your father told you?"

"Well, yes, but . . ."

"Uri, don't do it for your father."

"It's not for him; it's for the country."

The afternoon sun warmed their faces. "Maybe you'll change your mind," Mayim said, standing up. Uri reached for her, but she moved quickly up the stones beside the cave and started back up the wadi.

"Wait, Mayim."

"It's late. We have to go back now."

Even with the extra effort going uphill it took them less time to go back than it had taken them to climb down. When they reached the paved part of the path Knotty was coming down from the street.

"Here he is, Uri! You get to meet him at last."

Mayim ran uphill until she reached the knotted dog. Uri came right behind. When they met, the dog's tail was wagging and Mayim and Uri were laughing. Mayim put her arms around the dog's neck and hugged him. Uri tried to run his fingers through the dog's coat.

"No wonder you call him Knotty," he said.

"Doesn't he have a beautiful smile? And don't you love his pretty brown eyes?"

"He sure looks like he's smiling. Why is he so white around his mouth?"

"Because he's really old. See you later, Knotty," Mayim said, standing up.

The dog, still wagging his tail, continued on the path down the wadi.

Chapter Twelve

Chana made a light meal and in the early evening they all drove down to the train station. Chana waited in the car for Mayim to walk Uri to the train.

"Are you coming to Jerusalem for Yom Kippur?" Uri asked.

"Grandpa is coming to Aunt Yula's this year. The whole family will be here," Mayim answered.

"Oh," Uri said, disappointed.

"But after that I am sure we will come again very soon."

"At least for my Bar Mitzvah."

"I'm sure before that."

"Good-bye," Uri said, hesitated, put his hand on Mayim's shoulder and then kissed her lightly on the mouth.

Uri looked into Mayim's eyes a moment, to see if it was all right that he had kissed her. Mayim smiled, and Uri got on the train.

"Ima, Uri kissed me."

"I saw."

"Uri never kissed me before."

"I guess he's growing up."

Mayim daydreamed all through school on Sunday. A long silence brought her back to her classroom. Looking around Mayim realized all her classmates were watching her. Her teacher was sitting on the table in front of the class. He was waiting. He raised his eyebrows.

"What?" asked Mayim.

"Can you answer the question?"

Mayim started to ask what question, but had the presence of mind to shake her head no. And so the day went. Mayim walking in Hadar with all the young people and Uri. Mayim retracing all her steps with Uri down into the wadi. Mayim walking with Uri across the brown hills of Samaria which she had never seen.

Finally school was over, and Mayim slowly walked home alone. Mrs. Singer and Mr. Cohen were sitting in their rocking chairs on the patio of the old people's home as Mayim passed.

"Mayim," Mrs. Singer called Mayim over.

"How are you?" Mayim asked.

"Mr. Cohen wants to ask you a question."

"Yes?"

"This morning and then again this afternoon I saw a dog walking up and then back down the street. Mrs. Singer says that you know about him?"

"He lives down in the wadi. Uri and I hiked down the wadi yesterday and found the little cave he sleeps in."

"How long has he been here?" the old man asked.

"A really long time. Chaim, the butcher, who gives him his breakfast, says he was here when he came to Haifa. Why?"

"He reminds me of a dog that once belonged to a friend of mine. What is his name?"

"I call him Knotty. Actually everybody has their own name for him. Mrs. Koslovsky calls him Bailey. My Aunt Yula calls him Adel. Mr. Saludi calls him Laffah. But I think that Knotty has forgotten his name."

Mr. Cohen looked beyond Mayim down the street. "My friend's name was Yonah. I don't remember his dog's name."

"Where is your friend? Maybe he would like to come and see Knotty to see if it's his dog."

"My friend died in the war."

"Oh," Mayim said.

"The dog was with him. Yonah shielded the dog with his body when the firing started."

"He did that?' Mayim asked.

"That dog meant everything to him. When the Nazis came to his village in Hungary they killed his children, killed all the children and sent the parents to forced labor camps. His wife died of typhus. I think she died of a broken heart."

"Don't you think she's a little young to hear about this?" Mrs. Singer asked.

Mr. Cohen shook his head in disbelief at Mrs. Singer. "It's better that she knows. Besides she's a big girl."

"What happened after his wife died?" Mayim asked.

"He escaped from the camp and found his way through the forest and met some others Jews. They became partisans. They fought the Germans." Mr. Cohen stopped.

"Well?" asked Mayim, intense.

"So many stories of that time. Hard to keep them all

sorted out in my old mind." He thought a moment. "After the war ended he was smuggled into Israel with a few of the Jewish partisans. He was very sad. I remember a pale young man with no hope. We gave him the puppy to cheer him up. He loved that puppy. They went everywhere together. And when the war started here they went into battle together. After Yonah was killed the dog stayed with our unit, but when our position was overrun he disappeared. We all thought he had been killed."

"Maybe he ran away," Mayim suggested.

"Maybe."

"Do you really think Knotty was Yonah's dog?" Mayim asked.

"Wait, what war? How can it be the same dog, Mr. Cohen?" Mrs. Singer asked. "You were talking about the War of Independence, weren't you? I never heard of a dog living so long. It cannot be the same dog."

Mr. Cohen thought a moment and then said, "It must be another dog. But this dog is so much like Yonah's dog."

"Maybe he is the puppy of Yonah's dog," Mayim suggested. "And that is why they look alike."

Mr. Cohen nodded. "That must be the answer."

Chana waved to Mayim as she drove by in her car.

"I need to go now," Mayim said to Mr. Cohen. But can I come back another time?"

"You are always welcome, Mayim," Mrs. Singer said, smiling.

Mr. Cohen smiled and nodded.

•　　•　　•

"Ima, Mrs. Singer's new friend was just telling me the most amazing story!" Mayim shouted as she threw open the front door.

Chana laughed. "Mrs. Singer must be very happy, now that a man is living there."

"Ima, Mr. Cohen, Mrs. Singer's new friend, told me that he knew a dog that looked just like Knotty, and his owner, Yonah, was killed trying to save Knotty, or whatever his dog's name was, from the bullets during the war! Of course, it could be that this is only the son of that dog, but wouldn't it be wonderful if it were true and Knotty were Yonah's dog?"

Before Chana could open her mouth to say anything at all Mayim threw down her book bag and pulled out a pen and notebook. "I am going to write Uri. He will want to know the whole story."

Chapter Thirteen

The day before Yom Kippur Mayim went with Aunt Yula to Shouk Talpiyot to buy groceries. Mayim loved the shouk. On the street outside carts were piled high with melons. Wasps were eating from those cut in half. People shouted and moved quickly into the building. Mayim passed under a string of plucked turkeys hung upside down by their feet.

Aunt Yula bought potatoes and green beans and cucumbers. Next to the boxes full of tomatoes Mayim found muscat grapes, her favorite. Aunt Yula had to bargain for ten minutes to get a price she was willing to pay for them. At that, she bought only two small bunches.

Mayim followed her nose to her favorite part of the shouk, the spice seller. Great barrels of cumin and peppercorns and many shades of red and orange hot paprika were stacked in a row. She put her face into each barrel and breathed in the special scent of each spice. Aunt Yula laughed at her from across the narrow aisle at the olive seller's. She bought the wrinkled Greek olives Mayim loved, the ones packed in salt.

Aunt Yula bought onions from a man whose eyes were milky-blue. He carefully weighed the onions on his scale, touching all sides of the brass weights he put on the counterbalance. When Aunt Yula gave him the coins he touched each one carefully on both sides.

When all their salim were filled it was time to go. They couldn't carry any more. Aunt Yula stopped her car at the top of Rehov Margalit just across from the butcher shop. Mayim ran in and picked up a package of beef Aunt Yula had ordered. Just as she was about to leave she ran back and told Chaim about her hike down the wadi, about how she and Uri had found the little cave where Knotty slept. Chaim nodded. Aunt Yula pushed the horn, and Mayim hurried out to the car.

•   •   •

Grandpa arrived in the early evening and played shesbesh with Mayim until late into the night.

•   •   •

On Yom Kippur the day came sunny and hot. Mayim, Chana, and Grandpa joined Yula and her two sons, Moshe and David, and their wives.

"Moshe, I went down into the wadi and found a cave where Knotty lives."

"You mean that old Canaani that hangs around here begging for scraps?" Moshe asked. He had dark curly hair like Aunt Yula, but his features were like his father's.

"No!" Aunt Yula protested. "He is not Canaani, not a wild dog. He is a gentleman dog. And he never begs. He asks politely."

Moshe laughed, "Okay, Momma. A gentleman dog."

Mrs. Koslovsky arrived with a bottle of sweet vermouth. Mayim helped Aunt Yula take down the small crystal goblets from the cabinet in the dining room.

"Do I get any?" she asked Aunt Yula.

"Yes," said Aunt Yula, pouring her a quarter-inch in the bottom of a goblet. "But just a taste." Mayim took her sweet vermouth and squeezed in between Grandpa and Moshe on the sofa. She loved when the family was together. It was like being in a forest, safe in the branches of the oldest trees. And she loved all their voices, the different ways Moshe and David laughed. She put the goblet to her mouth and let the sweet vermouth touch her lips. Then she tasted her lips. Sweet vermouth was good. It made her tongue warm. She took another taste, and it made her throat warm.

Just as Mayim was taking her third sip the air raid siren went off. Everyone looked up.

"How can they be having an air raid warning on Yom Kippur?" Mrs. Koslovsky asked.

Grandpa went to the door. An Egged bus roared down Rehov Margalit.

"It's Yossi, the neighbor," Aunt Yula said. "Where is he going?"

"Turn on the radio," Mrs. Koslovsky. When Moshe turned the switch music was playing.

"Something is very wrong," Grandpa said. "The radio is always turned off on Yom Kippur."

The phone rang. Aunt Yula picked up the receiver and listened. Grim, she said, "The Syrians in the north and the Egyptians in the south."

"And the Jordanians?" asked David.

"She doesn't know," Aunt Yula answered.

"I have to call Jerusalem," Grandpa said.

Mayim went out to the patio. Several more cars raced down the street. Mayim listened. She heard explosions from artillery shells coming from just north of the city. Very close. The phone rang. Moshe's reserve unit was being called up. David's was on alert and would be called up in just a few hours.

Aunt Yula kissed Moshe and David good-bye. Mrs. Koslovsky went home to use her telephone.

"Maybe they are just shelling the border," Mayim said to her as she went out the patio gate.

"That's a hopeful thought." She did not smile.

"Do you hear the guns?" Mayim asked, pointing to the sky.

Mrs. Koslovsky listened. "It sounds like our cousins are shooting at us again. Go inside, Mayim. I'll be back."

Mayim found Aunt Yula washing the goblets in the kitchen sink. She sat on the bench next to the table and pulled her knees up. She could hear her mother and Grandpa speaking softly in the bedroom.

Yula leaned her forearms against the edge of the sink. "Always more and more blood for this country," she said to herself, to the goblets, to the water running in the sink.

What the sound of cannon fire had not brought, Aunt Yula's words did. Terror. Mayim jumped down from the kitchen table and threw open the bedroom door intending to throw herself into Grandpa's arms. When she saw her mother's face she stopped. She looked at her Grandpa. She saw the fear in her heart reflected in both of their faces. And that fear sank into her feet and into the earth. She couldn't do it. She couldn't be a baby anymore. They needed her to be strong. Not to cry. To be brave. To help them be brave.

"What's going to happen now?" she asked, her voice quiet.

Chana said, "Mayim, Grandpa has to get back to Jerusalem. There will be a bus later on, but just one bus to Jerusalem. I will have to drive him down to the Ir to get that bus, and you will have to stay here with Aunt Yula."

"Why doesn't Grandpa take our car?" Mayim suggested.

"You might need the car," Grandpa answered.

Aunt Yula made them dinner with the vegetables from Shouk Talpiyot. To Mayim their walk through the shouk already seemed centuries away. She cut the triangular plastic milk bag, put it into the blue holder and put it on the table.

"Mayim, close the tressim and turn off all of the lights," Chana said after dinner. "I want you to stay inside until I get back."

"Take this," Aunt Yula said, passing Chana a sheet of dark transparent blue plastic. "For the headlights."

Grandpa and Chana drove off into the dark evening. Mayim slipped outside to the patio and listened to the voices coming from the synagogue. It was Yom Kippur. The Day of Atonement. A terrible day for an attack, everyone at home. No one listening to the radio or television.

Overhead one came and then another—fighter jets heading north to fight the Syrians. On the ground Moshe and David, in their tanks, heading south. Mayim listened to the guns until her mother came back.

Chapter Fourteen

Mayim woke up in her own bed. Her mother was up listening to the radio.

"Is there any news?" Mayim asked.

"Very little more than we knew last night. I am going over to Aunt Yula's for a minute to see if she has heard anything."

"Why don't you just call her?" Mayim asked, uneasy about being left alone.

"The government has asked everyone not to use the telephones right now. Only for emergencies. I'll be right back. Why don't you get dressed."

When Mayim was brushing her teeth the phone rang.

"Mayim?"

"Yes, who is this?"

"This is Chaim."

"Chaim?"

"Listen, my reserve unit has been called up. I'm leaving in just a few minutes. There is something you need to do."

"What?'

"You must feed Havi."

"Knotty?"

"Knotty, yes. He will be too scared to come up from the wadi because of the guns and all the planes. You have to take him some food every day. He's a very old dog now. My uncle will be here in the shop and will give you the food, but you are the only one who knows where his cave is."

"I can't go down there by myself," Mayim protested.

"Mayim, the dog needs you. He will be too scared to leave the cave."

"Maybe he won't be scared."

"Mayim, listen to me. During the Six Day War, Havi, or Knotty, didn't come back up the wadi until after the war was over and I went down to him. He is terrified when all the people are scared. He is too old now to go very long without food. Please, Mayim. I love this dog. Please, will you take care of him?"

"All right," Mayim answered quietly. "But my mother

won't let me go by myself."

"Don't tell her."

"What if I get in trouble."

"Put all the blame on me. If she finds out, tell her I made you do it. Then she won't be angry at you. I have to go now, Mayim."

"Wait, Chaim, where are you going?"

"You know I cannot tell you."

"Be careful. Call me as soon as you get back."

"I will Mayim. Thank you for taking care of Havi. It means a lot to me not to have to be worrying about him."

"Don't worry. I'm sure the war will be over in just a few days."

"From your mouth to God's ears. Please, Mayim say a prayer for us."

"Okay," Mayim whispered into the telephone.

Mayim went to her mother's dresser and opened the top drawer. Inside were things that had belonged to her father. Next to his watch she found it. A square piece of tin, half of her father's dog tag. The other half they had buried with her father. This half they had broken off and given to her mother. Funny, she thought, this small piece of metal still exists, but my father doesn't. The square Hebrew letters struck in the metal spelled out his name. Gershon Dagan. There were numbers, but they meant nothing to Mayim. She slipped the piece of tin with her father's name into a small leather pouch. She found a piece of string in the kitchen and tied a loop to the pouch. She slipped the string over her head and put the leather pouch under her shirt.

She packed a bag of cheese and bread and took a plastic bottle full of water. On top she wedged in a metal bowl. On the table she left a note saying that she had gone up to see Mrs. Singer and Mr. Cohen.

Mayim crossed on the far side of the street. In case her mother should come up from Aunt Yula's she would be less likely to be seen. Halfway down the paved path Mayim stopped to listen. Silence. The city was quiet. In the distance Mayim could no longer hear the cannon firing. She raced down to the end of the paved path and started zigzagging along the path she and Uri had taken. When she came to the place where she had slipped before she went around and came back. She found her way quickly as if she had been in the wadi a hundred times before instead of one trip up and one trip down. When she arrived at the rocky overhang she called out and looked over, trying to see the ledge below. She worked her way down the rocky staircase. Knotty was not on the ledge. She took off her pack and crawled into the cave. Knotty sat up. He was shaking all over.

"Oh, my poor Knotty," Mayim said, putting her arms around his neck. "Please don't be scared. Nothing can hurt you down here. And until you aren't scared anymore I will come every day and bring your food."

Mayim poured water for Knotty in the metal bowl and set it outside on the ledge.

"Come out here," Mayim called.

Knotty pressed himself far into the back of the cave and whined.

"Do you want some cheese?"

Knotty turned around but did not come any closer to the opening of the cave. Mayim took the cheese and bread from her knapsack and held it out to the dog.

Knotty sniffed, but wouldn't eat.

"Please Knotty. Eat a little," Mayim said and broke off a small piece of cheese. She pushed it in the dog's mouth and he ate it. Piece by piece Mayim fed the cheese and bread to the dog. When she was finished he was still shaking.

"I'll put your water bowl inside," Mayim said. She rubbed the top of his head and kissed his muzzle. "I have to go, but I'll be right back. Tomorrow I'll come back. I'll come with some more food. Please don't be so scared."

Chapter Fifteen

Chana was on the phone when Mayim arrived home.

"How is Mrs. Singer doing?" Chana asked, putting down the receiver.

"Fine. Who was on the telephone?"

"The secretary at the Technion. They have canceled classes. Most of the students and the professors have been called up with their units. And for the same reason there will be no school. The teachers at your school were all called up, too."

"No school?" Mayim said.

"I want you to run up to the mecolit and see if we can get some milk and bread from the grocer. Mrs. Koslovsky was at the Super Sol in the Merkaz, and the shelves are almost empty. She said she had to wait two hours in line to get a small package of beans."

"The Super Sol is empty?"

"Mayim, people are hoarding. It makes things much

more difficult. Please run up to the mecolit."

"Okay. Did Grandpa call?"

"Yes, he's fine. Go and when you come back we can talk about what Grandpa said."

Chana gave Mayim a small purse and a sal to carry the groceries back. When she got to the mecolit a woman was inside arguing with the grocer. "I can only give you what I have," he said, gesturing with his hands.

"You are saving it for someone else!" the woman shouted and ran out of the door.

"Hello, Mayim," said the grocer.

"Mother needs some bread and milk."

"Mayim. Listen to me. I am only giving milk to families with children. Maybe tomorrow we will get another delivery, but who can say. So many people have been called up with their units, there is no one to work." The grocer wrapped the triangular plastic milk bags in newspaper and put it in her sal. "I don't want any of the neighbors to see I gave you milk. I don't want any more fights." He slipped a loaf of bread in her sal. Mayim gave him a bill, and he gave her back coins in change.

On the street Mayim met Mrs. Koslovsky.

"Good, I'm glad you got a few things," she said. "I went to the Super Sol this morning, and it was bedlam. The civilian population has a hard time adjusting to the privations of war."

"What will we do?" Mayim asked.

"We don't have to do anything. Sit tight. The soldiers are doing everything. If we see Arabs moving down the streets with guns drawn then we'll have to do something."

"That's not going to happen," Mayim said. "The army will never let that happen."

"You'd better pray it doesn't happen. Keep your eyes open, girl."

• • •

Chana was listening to the radio when Mayim came into the kitchen. Mayim put the milk away. The Prime Minister's voice was paced, even, angry.

"We have broken through the Syrian lines, and they are in retreat," the Prime Minister claimed.

"That's good, Ima; then the war will end very soon," Mayim said.

Chana switched off the radio. She did not smile.

Mayim took a breath. "What did Grandpa say?"

"We are losing many pilots. It's terrible, Mayim."

"How? Our pilots are the best in the world! No one can beat them!

"The Arabs are shooting them down with anti-aircraft missiles. The pilots don't have a chance. Grandpa says it will be a long war. Listen, Mayim. I can't tell you any more. I shouldn't have told you that. Nothing Grandpa tells us can go outside of this house to anyone."

"You know you can trust me, I'm grown up now." Mayim said.

"It's better that the people don't know what is happening. It's better that they go on with their lives and let the army worry about the war."

• • •

In the evening a phone call came from Uri. "Are you all right?" he asked Mayim.

"Of course I'm all right. We are not supposed to use the phone, except in emergencies."

"I know."

"Was your father called up?"

"Yes. Mother is very anxious, but I'm not afraid. The army will push the Syrians all the way back to Damascus. Then we will take Damascus."

"A lot of people will die."

"Only the Syrians will die. It will be like before—the Arab soldiers will run out of their shoes when our tanks come."

Mayim wanted to tell him about the pilots, about all the pilots dying, shot down in their planes, but she kept her promise and remained quiet.

Uri went on, "After this war we will have all the land between the Nile and the Euphrates. It will be holy land. Our holy land. And the Arabs will all be gone."

"But how many Israelis will die for this land?"

"What is the matter with you? Why are you being so negative?"

"Uri, I'm not negative. I just don't agree with you." As soon as the words left her mouth she wished she hadn't spoken them.

"I am not going to listen to this. I am not speaking to you, Mayim. Whose side are you on anyway?" Uri hung up the phone.

• • •

"I fought with Uri today," Mayim told Mrs. Koslovsky. "I don't know what's the matter with him. He gets so angry if I disagree with him at all. He says we are going to take Damascus."

"It's a long way to Damascus."

"He says we are going to take all the land between the Nile and the Euphrates. He says it will be our holy land."

"God makes the land holy. How can the bottoms of our feet make it any more holy than the bottoms of Arab feet? At any rate it's going to be a job just getting Kuneitra back."

"The Arabs have Kuneitra?" Mayim gasped.

"You didn't hear me say that. And I don't want anyone to hear you say that. That's top secret, my dear."

The air raid siren wailed down Rehov Margalit.

"Should we go to the shelter at the neighbors'?" Mayim asked, looking through the door at the night sky. Mrs. Koslovsky's building was old and had no underground shelter.

99

"Six of the one, half a dozen of the other."

"What does that mean?"

"The shelter in the apartment building isn't reinforced enough to take a direct hit. If there was a direct hit, all the cement would come down on our heads. If we are upstairs and lucky we'd just be blown out through the window." Mrs. Koslovsky smiled ironically.

"But the tressim are closed," Mayim said. "Maybe we should open them."

Mrs. Koslovsky switched off the lamp next to the couch, and Mayim pulled the strap raising the heavy metal tressim. They stood in the doorway to the balcony and listened. The air raid siren stopped and the city was silent.

Half an hour later the all-clear sounded, and Mayim raced across the street to her home.

Chapter Sixteen

The air raid siren awakened Mayim twice in the night. She went to her mother's room the first time.

"Should we go across to the shelter?"

"I think it will be all right. Why don't you sleep here," her mother said.

Mayim lay awake listening to the sounds of the night. She was still awake when the all-clear wailed over the sleeping city. She thought about Uri, about all the things she could say to him, the things she could have said to him if he hadn't hung up on her. She decided to say them the next time. If there would be a next time. Just as she slipped into the part of her mind where words made their own life, their own world, the air raid siren ripped open that world. Mayim slept only a few minutes after dawn.

Chana drove to the Technion to lock up the lab and make sure all the chemicals were stored away. Mayim hurried over to the butcher's to get some meat scraps from

Chaim's uncle. On the way back she stopped at the mecol-it and asked for eggs. There were no eggs. All the eggs had been shipped up to the Golan and down to the Sinai to feed the soldiers.

Mayim packed a lunch for Knotty of bread and meat and a full bottle of cool water. She thought about leaving a note for her mother but decided against it. She would get back before her mother and wouldn't have to tell any lies.

She found the dog with his nose between his front paws on the ledge in front of the small cave. He didn't get up when she stepped down to the ledge. She poured water into his metal bowl and was about to take out his lunch when the air raid siren howled over the city.

Knotty jumped up and ran to the back of his cave. He pressed himself against the back wall and panted heavily. Mayim followed him into the cave and put her arms around his neck. His entire body shook, and she rubbed his back and tried to soothe him. She pushed him down and lay with her body close to his.

"Please, God, bring peace to this dog. And peace to the land," Mayim prayed.

After a while he stopped shaking, but his body continued shivering off and on. He stopped panting. He stopped shivering for several minutes, and Mayim fell asleep with her arms around him.

·   ·   ·

At first the sound came from far away. Maybe it was the phone ringing. No, it was someone singing. It was Chana singing. Mayim lay nestled next to her mother. And he was there stroking Mayim's hair off her forehead, listening to the lovely sounds of his wife singing. And Mayim turned and looked at her father's face, and he smiled back at her and kissed her cheek. And it was her father's face, the brown eyes, the funny fat nose Mayim loved to pinch, and the curly beard of red and black and blonde hairs she could never resist pulling. And she pulled it, and her father cried out louder than he needed to, laughing, and Chana sang louder trying not to laugh. And the sound was louder and louder.

It was the all-clear. And Mayim was awake. She closed her eyes and let her father's face fill her mind. The sound of his laughter filled her ears. The touch of his beard tight in her fingers, how could she have ever forgotten it? She pressed her face against his chest and remembered exactly how he smelled. She went back one more time, to listen, to touch and then she lifted her head off Knotty's neck. She could wake up now. She would never forget him again.

Mayim coaxed Knotty to the ledge and hand fed him. He took the meat eagerly and drank some water from his metal bowl.

·   ·   ·

Mayim closed the door to her bedroom just as her mother opened the front door.

"Mayim, I forgot. Would you please run up to the mecolit and get some eggs. I meant to stop and I forgot," Chana called from the hall.

Mayim stepped out of her room. She considered telling her there were no eggs, but then she would have to explain her trip to the mecolit. Better not to tell, she decided.

"Okay, Ima."

"Take my change purse."

·   ·   ·

Mayim sat on the corner outside the mecolit with her chin in her hands and elbows on her knees. She wished the war would end. She wished her father hadn't died. She wished there wouldn't be any more wars.

"Mayim, did you need something?" asked the grocer.

"No. I was just sitting. I don't suppose any eggs came in?"

"Mayim, I told you this morning. We won't have any eggs for a long time."

"Okay."

Mayim got up and went back down Rehov Margalit. Mr. Cohen sat alone on the patio with a shawl around his shoulders. Mayim slowed her step and looked closely to see if he was asleep. Mr. Cohen raised his head and smiled.

"Boker tov," he said.

"Boker tov," Mayim answered. "How are you feeling?"

"It is a beautiful day. What more does a person need?"

"Eggs. We need eggs. We need the soldiers to come home. We need the war to stop."

"These things will happen," he said.

"When?"

"When God wills it."

"God," Mayim said. The word opened a room inside her that was empty.

"Maybe you should say a prayer," suggested Mr. Cohen.

"Okay," Mayim answered quietly. She turned to go down the street.

"I remembered."

"What? What did you remember?"

"The name. The name my friend gave his dog."

"What, what was it?" Mayim asked urgently.

"Kayori."

"I've never heard of that name before."

"It's Yiddish. It means dawn. That's what my friend called his little puppy, Kayori. You can try this name. See if he answers to it. If he is the same dog, he will remember, I am sure."

"But what if he has forgotten his name?"

"If he forgot, then he can remember."

"Hello, Mayim," Mrs. Singer said coming outside with a tray filled with teacups. "Would you like to join us for tea?"

"My mother is waiting for me. Maybe tomorrow afternoon."

"We would be delighted to have you as our guest," Mr. Cohen said.

Chapter Seventeen

Chana and Mayim went to see Aunt Yula after dinner. They watched television. Henry Kissinger, the American Secretary of State, was interviewed. He called for an immediate end to the fighting.

"I hope he doesn't sell us down the river," Aunt Yula said.

"Why would he do that?" Mayim asked.

"Trying to prove to the Americans that he isn't a Jew," she replied.

Mayim watched films of Israeli prisoners-of-war captured on the Golan.

"What do you think happened to Talya and Ronit?" she suddenly asked her mother.

Chana put her hand over her mouth and shook her head.

Mayim slipped her nightgown over her head just as the phone rang.

It was Uri.

"Mayim?"

"Hello," Mayim answered.

"I am sorry," he said. "I am sorry I got angry and hung up on you. I hope you are not still angry at me."

"I was never angry at you. I don't know why you were so angry at me."

"I am sorry. Please, I won't ever do that again."

"Okay."

"So how are you?" he asked.

"Just waiting. And you?"

"Mayim, I went to the hospital tonight," Uri said slowly.

"What happened?" Mayim asked with concern.

"Nothing really. I fell on the steps down to the shelter during the air raid. Some children were running, and I lost my step. My mother thought I might have broken my wrist, so after the all-clear we went to the hospital for x-rays."

"Did you break your wrist?"

"No, as it turned out, it was a sprain. I have a splint to wear for a few weeks, that's all."

"I'm so glad, Uri. Does it hurt?"

"Not really. Not any more." He was silent for a moment.

"Uri?" Mayim asked. "Are you there?"

He went on, "There was a man in the emergency room who came in right after me. He died of a heart attack. They couldn't do anything to save him. And the whole time I was watching the doctors try to save him, I kept thinking why am I here? I shouldn't be taking up anybody's time. There is nothing wrong with me." Uri spoke slowly. He was quiet again for a moment and then went on. "Mayim, there were two soldiers in the hall when I left. The nurse was helping them walk. They both had bandages around their heads. They were blind, Mayim. Two tank commanders both blinded from the anti-tank weapons the Egyptians used against them. They will never be able to see again. They were young men, Mayim."

Mayim didn't answer. She just looked at the black receiver near her mouth.

"I don't like this war," Uri said, quiet.

"I think a lot of soldiers are dying," Mayim answered.

"I have to go now."

"Good-bye, Uri."

"Good-bye."

Mayim put the receiver down. She went into the kitchen where her mother was putting away the last of the dishes.

"Who was that?' Chana asked.

"Uri. Uri is very sad about the war."

"Everybody is very sad about the war."

Mayim was still awake when the phone rang again. Her mother answered it and came to her room.

"Mayim, Aunt Yula just heard on the news. There will be school tomorrow."

"School?" Mayim asked. "Is the war over?"

"Not yet, but it is time to go back to school. There will be many substitute teachers, but it's better for everyone if the children are in school."

"Oh," Mayim said.

•　　•　　•

In the morning she got up early and ran to the wadi.

"Knotty!" she called. She raced down to the bottom of the paved path. "Knotty!" She knew it would be impossible to go down to the wadi after school with her mother

111

home. The dog had to come up to get his food and water. She ran back and forth calling a few times.

"Bailey!"

"Laffah!"

"Adel!"

"Havi!"

"Knotty, please come up. I have to go back to school now!"

Then she remembered what Mr. Cohen had told her.

"Kayori! Come here! Kayori! Please come here! Kayori!"

She waited a few moments and called again, "Kayori!" Her throat was beginning to get sore. She ran down the rocky part of the path and called again. "Kayori!"

She came to a spot where she could see the rocky over-hang above Knotty's cave. "Kayori!"

Then he was there, smiling. On the rocky outcrop the dog stood, his tail wagging.

"Come, Kayori!"

Mayim watched as the dog made his way straight up the wadi.

"Kayori, you remember! You remember!"

The dog raced up the hill and just before he reached Mayim he spun around like a puppy and put his chin down on his front paws. He did remember. He remembered his name. He remembered who he was. And he was happy. He danced around Mayim, and together they ran up the wadi.

Chapter Eighteen

Mrs. Koslovsky was outside watering her garden. "Good morning, Mayim." She spoke to Mayim through the pomegranate trees. "I heard a rumor that school was going to resume today."

Mayim ignored her remark. "Guess what?"

"Mayim, I am too old for guessing games this early in the morning."

Mayim ran around the pomegranate trees to the garden steps. When she came up the stairs the dog was right behind her.

"Look," Mayim said standing aside so Mrs. Koslovsky could see the dog.

"How did you get him up out of the wadi?"

"I called him by his real name, and he was so happy to hear it after so many years of not remembering that he bounced straight up the wadi like a gazelle."

Mrs. Koslovsky turned off the water to the garden hose.

"Good morning, Bailey," she said to the dog.

"It's Kayori. Call him Kayori."

"Well I don't know if I want to. He's been Bailey for ever so many years."

"Please."

"Mrs. Koslovsky put her hands on her hips. "Good morning, Kayori."

The knotted dog spun in a circle on his hind feet and barked, his tail moving as fast as it could. Mrs. Koslovsky laughed out loud.

"Kayori!" she shouted and the dog put his front feet on her shoulders.

"You see," Mayim said.

"Let's not take liberties with my good nature," Mrs. Koslovsky said pushing the dog down. "Did you call him every name in the universe until you found Kayori?"

"Oh, no, Mrs. Koslovsky."

"Come inside and tell me then. We'll put together a nice breakfast for Kayori." Mayim told the story Mr. Cohen had told her about his friend from Hungary as they broke pieces of challah off into a bowl.

Mrs. Koslovsky regarded the dog closely. "Get some

cheese from the refrigerator." She sat down on a kitchen chair and looked at Kayori's old white face. "Kayori," she spoke the name quietly. The dog slipped his chin onto Mrs. Koslovsky`s knee and looked into her eyes. "I can see this is the name he wants."

"I helped him remember it."

"That's a very special gift, Mayim," Mrs. Koslovsky said, stroking the knotted hair back from Kayori's eyes.

"And you know what he gave me?"

Mrs. Koslovsky raised her eyebrows.

"My father. He gave me back my father." Mayim told her about the dream she had in the cave.

"You have given each other treasures."

•　　•　　•

By the end of the week everybody on Rehov Margalit was calling the dog Kayori. Aunt Yula was very sad to have to give up the name, Adel, but it was apparent to all that Kayori was his true name.

Several days later Henry Kissinger convinced the American president to resupply the Israeli army. With the new planes and tanks they pushed the Syrians off the

Golan and in the south surrounded the Egyptian army. In another week a cease-fire was called, and when Mayim heard the news she took her father's dog tag from around her neck and slipped it back into the drawer.

Chaim, the butcher, came home a week after that. Kayori danced circles around Chaim and after that Chaim never called him anything but Kayori.

•   •   •

Shortly after the cease-fire, Mr. Saludi began making his daily trips to Rehov Margalit again, bringing fruits and vegetables.

"We solved the mystery," Mayim told Mr. Saludi early one morning on her way to school.

Mr. Saludi smiled after hearing Mayim tell the story about the knotted dog.

"Will you call him Kayori, too?" Mayim asked.

"If it pleases you."

Chapter Nineteen

It snowed in Jerusalem that long cold winter. Mayim had never seen snow. Aunt Yula taught her how to knit and together they knitted up piles of balaclavas to keep the soldiers warm up on Mount Hermon where they kept guard at the cease-fire lines.

• • •

On a late February afternoon Mayim sat on the patio in a sunny spot against the stone wall with Kayori. She broke pieces of salty cheese into little balls and fed them to the dog one at a time. Kayori put his chin on Mayim's knee when he was finished eating.

"Are you going to see Mrs. Koslovsky now?" Mayim asked.

Kayori wagged his tail, and he ambled up to the gate and through to the street.

"Say hi for me," Mayim called after him. She picked up

her notebook and pen and began to complete her extra-credit science assignment for school. She had made a list of all the birds she had seen in Ahuza, her neighborhood, and down in the wadi. For each species she noted how many individuals she had seen and whether they were male or female. She took her colored pencils and added color to the sketches she had made. She hoped her teacher would like her report. She could use the extra points to make up for the electricity unit she had done so badly in. After considering a moment, it occurred to her that she didn't have to turn it in to her teacher. It could be the beginning of a longer project, a project just for herself, something she could work on over the summer as well.

Mayim looked up to see two people step down from the sidewalk.

"Hi, Mayim, do you remember us?"

"Ronit! Talya!" Mayim shouted, jumping up. She threw her arms around both of them.

"Be careful," Talya said, holding a small sack high over Mayim's head. "You'll break them."

"I'm sorry."

Talya brought the paper sack down in front of Mayim

and folded the paper edges back. There were three eggs inside.

"Betzim," Mayim whispered, the first ones she had seen since the war began.

"My mother's cousin lives on a moshav and she got a whole flat of eggs from him. I was sure your mother would want a few."

Mayim raced to the front door. "Ima! Ronit and Talya are here. They are alive! And Ima, they have eggs for us!"

"This is so very nice," Chana said. "We were really worried about what might have happened to you."

"I told you she would remember us," Ronit said to Talya.

"Come inside and tell us all about what happened up on the Golan," Chana said. She mixed some soda drinks and put out a few vanilla biscuits.

"We were evacuated with the civilians just after the Syrians started shelling our positions. Three of the guys from our unit were killed trying to keep the Syrian army from sweeping down into the Galilee. Ours was lucky, other units lost many more soldiers. There just weren't enough tanks to hold them back."

"And because of the anti-aircraft missiles we couldn't get air support. At one point the first night there were six Israeli tanks holding off hundreds of Syrian tanks."

"Oo ah," Chana said, hand to her mouth. "We had no idea things were so bad."

"Reinforcements didn't get up there until the next afternoon."

"I don't understand," Chana said. "You can drive to the Golan in a few hours."

"Nobody understands. The army was not prepared. Why? I don't know. But I am sure we will find out."

"Are you on leave now?" Mayim asked.

"For a few days, then we'll go back. It's a little boring since the cease-fire, but nobody dies."

"Do you think the cease-fire will hold?" Mayim asked. Ronit nodded. "I hope."

• • •

The cease-fire did hold and in March Aunt Yula, both her sons and their wives, Mrs. Koslovsky, Chana, and Mayim made the journey to Jerusalem where they all celebrated Uri Urlansky's Bar Mitzvah.

Mayim stood on the balcony overlooking Jerusalem the next morning. The green hills were blanketed with wild mustard flowers.

"Grandpa, do you think that Kayori is really the real Kayori?"

Grandpa was silent looking at the clouds over the city.

"I mean could a dog be so old? And if it is the real Kayori, how did he stay alive so long?"

"Maybe after his friend was killed he needed to find someone else. Another troubled heart he could bring peace to. Maybe it was the only way he could become who he really is."

"Do you think he is now who he really is?" Mayim asked.

Grandpa laughed. "Yes."

"And you know what else, Grandpa?"

"What?"

"So am I."

Chapter Twenty

Uri helped Mayim load the car for the trip back to Haifa.

"Do you feel older?" Mayim asked.

Uri laughed. "No. Well, yes. Actually, no. You met Elie, right?"

Mayim nodded, "He's your mother's youngest brother who lives in Boston."

"I am going to stay with him this summer."

"What?"

"My mother asked him if I could come. She thinks it would be good for me to go outside of the country, to see more."

"Your mother?" Mayim asked, surprised.

"Boston University has special classes in the summer for kids who are really good at math and science. My Uncle Elie says it will give me more to think about before I decide what to do with my life. And, of course, my

English will get better."

Mayim looked at Uri. "Good. Will you write to me? I will want to know everything."

"I will write every day."

•   •   •

A week before summer Mayim walked home, trying to imagine what Uri's summer studies would be like.

"Mayim."

Mayim turned and looked back over her shoulder.

"Mr. Saludi, good afternoon."

"Good, I hoped I would find you now."

"School just let out."

"I know. I have a gift for you." Mr. Saludi reached inside the ragged bag on his shoulder and took out an old wooden box.

Mayim looked at the box and at Mr. Saludi. She could not imagine what might be inside. She could not imagine what he would give her.

"Come and sit, I will show you."

Mayim slipped her book bag down to the sidewalk and wiggled onto the stone wall. Mr. Saludi sat down next to her and placing the box on his knees lifted the thin wood-en lid.

"Ah!" Mayim said, taking in a breath. Under the lid carefully placed she saw several tiny bird nests. One nest had four dark, speckled eggs inside. Mr. Saludi took out a small bundle wrapped in a handkerchief. He passed it to Mayim. She opened the cloth carefully and inside found a collection of broken egg shells. Some were brown, some spotted. They were from many different species of birds.

"Where did you get these?" Mayim asked.

"They are from here," he said. "When I was a boy I knew every rock and every tree on Mount Carmel. This was where I came to spend my days. That was before all of this, before all these buildings were built. My family lived here before Israel became a state. Soon after the soldiers came and made us leave Mount Carmel. All the people in my village were moved down to Wadi Nisnas near Khuri Street."

"Is that where you live now?" Mayim asked.

"Yes, with my children and my grandchildren."

"I never knew where you lived," Mayim said.

"I want you to have these things, Mayim. I saw you

drawing the birds one morning last week. Look here." He folded up the handkerchief of broken shells and put it back. He lifted up one of the nests and underneath were many feathers laid side-by-side.

"Don't you have someone to give them to?"

"You are someone."

"But what about your children."

"They are all grown up."

"Your grandchildren?"

"They don't think any of this is real. They only care about the television, about politics," he said looking at the box. "To know the world, to really know it, you have to bring something to it. Something from yourself." He put his fists on his chest and then opened his hands out to touch the air.

Mr. Saludi closed the box. He stood up and handed it to Mayim. "It is the greatest of pleasures to bestow this gift upon you."

Mayim stood down from the wall and accepted his gift.

GLOSSARY

Ahuza:	Mayim's neighborhood in Haifa situated on Mount Carmel between the Merkaz HaCarmel and the University of Haifa
Balaclava:	A close-fitting woolen cap that covers the head and neck, but not the face
Bar mitzvah:	Ceremony to celebrate the age of inclusion in the religious life of the Jewish community
Bedhouin:	Nomadic Arabs of the desert
Betzim:	Eggs
Boker tov:	The greeting, "good morning"
Canaani:	The wild dogs of Israel
Carmelit:	The underground subway that runs between the harbor level of the city of Haifa or the Ir, to the

	second level of Hadar, and up to the third level of Mount Carmel
Falafel:	A middle eastern sandwich made of fried ground chickpeas inserted in a pita on a bed of shredded lettuce and tomatoes, garnished with tehina and hot sauce
Gan yeledim:	Nursery school
Hadar:	The middle level of the city of Haifa
Hafsakat tzohorayim:	The formal afternoon rest period taken between two and four o'clock in the afternoon. Even if the children don't sleep they have to be quiet so the adults can rest.
Hamseen:	The hot desert winds that blow off the desert towards the Mediterranean sea
Harif:	A red, spicy sauce used to flavor falafels and tehina
Ima:	Mother

Ir:	The lowest level of the city of Haifa, located at sea level
Keffiyah:	A folded, cloth head covering worn by Arabs
Matzo:	Unleavened wheat crackers
Merkaz HaCarmel:	The commercial district of Mount Carmel
Mecolit:	A very small "mom and pop" corner grocery store
Moshe Dayan:	The Israeli general serving as the Minister of Defense under the government of Prime Minister Golda Meir
Mitz escholiot:	A soda drink made with seltzer water added to a concentrated grapefruit syrup
Pita:	A hollow, round, wheat bread used for making falafels
Rehov:	Street
Salim (sal):	Plastic net bags for carrying groceries
Schnitzel:	A fried Israeli dish made with

	breaded chicken breast
Shabat shalom:	Sabbath greeting
Shalom:	A greeting, "hello" or "good-bye." Also means "peace"
Shawerma:	A Middle-Eastern sandwich made from grilled and spiced layers of turkey or lamb, usually served in a pita
Shesbesh:	A board game, backgammon
Shouk Talpiyot:	Central market in Haifa. Part of the market is inside a building and many vendors set up baskets outside along the street.
Technion:	The Israel Institute of Technology, the oldest university in the country
Tehina:	Sesame-seed paste eaten on a plate, on falafel, or shawerma
Tressim:	Slatted window shutters. They can be raised partially to allow air to blow through the slats, or raised completely above the window.

Villa:	A detached house. Most Israelis live in apartments.
Wadi:	A ravine or an arroyo, formed by flash floods
Yom Kippur:	The Day of Atonement, the holiest Jewish holiday